Sassy Uncovers Peter Allen's Secret

Sassy Uncovers Peter Allen's Secret

B.A. Johnson

Fresh Ink Group
Guntersville

Sassy Uncovers Peter Allen's Secret

Copyright © 2021
by B. A. Johnson
All rights reserved

Fresh Ink Group
An Imprint of:
The Fresh Ink Group, LLC
1021 Blount Avenue #931
Guntersville, AL 35976
Email: info@FreshInkGroup.com
FreshInkGroup.com

Edition 1.0 2022

Edited by Stephen Geez / FIG
Art by Anik / FIG
Author Photo by BPO+Digital Media
Author's Makeup by Shan-Lo Makeup, LLC
Book design by Amit Dey / FIG
Cover design by Stephen Geez / FIG

Cataloging-in-Publication Recommendations:
JUV011010 JUVENILE FICTION / People & Places / United States / African American & Black
REL091000 RELIGION / Christian Education / Children & Youth
JUV033240 JUVENILE FICTION / Religious / Christian / Values & Virtues

Library of Congress Control Number: 2022921493

ISBN-13: 978-1-947893-78-8 Papercover
ISBN-13: 978-1-947893-85-6 Hardcover
ISBN-13: 978-1-947893-86-3 Ebooks

Sassy Uncovers Peter Allen's Secret is dedicated to Reverend Mark Kelly Tyler, PhD, Senior Pastor of Mother Bethel African Methodist Episcopal Church in Philadelphia, Pennsylvania. Dr. Tyler's research on the life of Peter Allen inspired the writing of this story.

This book is also dedicated to Mrs. Ollye Conley, a noted Huntsville historian who introduced me to the history of Peter Allen and shared Dr. Tyler's research.

Acknowledgements

I am continually inspired to write by my significant other, my family, my close friends, and other writers. I'm grateful to each for allowing me the time and space to collect my thoughts, be as creative as possible, and spend countless hours with my laptop instead of them. The support and encouragement of my fellow published author friends, Mrs. Barbara Bradford Mostella and Mrs. Ecleave Jackson, compelled me to finish this book. My beta readers—Ms. Lady Hereford, Dr. Thalia Love-Brown, Dr. Janice Draper-Toney, Ms. Paula Pippen, and Mrs. Kay Adkins—provided priceless assistance. Thank you, ladies, for taking the time to read and give very helpful feedback. The St. John African Methodist Episcopal Church family and members of the AME church worldwide are some of my most enthusiastic fans, people whose patronage I greatly appreciate.

Lastly, I am thankful to my talented editor, Stephen Geez, who helped keep my characters in the right tense and place, and had them say the right things when the time was right. Anik is a gifted artist/illustrator, who can always bring to life the characters in my head and make them lifelike and likeable by kids of all ages.

This second book, *Sassy Uncovers Peter Allen's Secret*, was truly a labor of love for children everywhere, brought to fruition with the assistance of an outstanding publisher, Fresh Ink Group.

Preface

*H*ave you ever noticed the family on old church fans? Every church has them—fans, that is. The ushers usually pass them out at the door on hot summer Sundays or during funerals. The family looks like any other devout church members, but they have no names. Who are these people? They don't look like anybody at this church. By the age of ten, I decided to give them names and identities.

The little girl is Mary Margaret Fanson. You might know her from the fans in your church. Her dad and mom are Brock and Gloria Fanson. Her big brother is Franklin. During the week, they and their fan live in a storage unit with the *Holy Bible* and the church hymnal. On Sundays they come alive and jump off the fan to attend Big Morning Star African Methodist Episcopal (AME) Church. Mary Margaret's grandmother is not on the fan, but she lives with them, too. She's called Big Momma, not that she's big or anything, but she *is* older. Big Momma and Mary Margaret spend a lot of time together.

Big Momma thinks Sassy is smarter and more high-spirited than most little girls her age, which is why she calls her Sassy. The Fansons are members of Big Morning Star. They are proud AMEs. Sassy boasts that she has been attending that church all her life. She's ten years old, so that's a long time.

Last year in Children's Church, Sassy learned the history of the AME Church. She was very excited to finally understand why Big Momma is so thrilled to be a member. Sassy and Big Momma would sit on the patio, eat sugar cookies, and drink lemonade while Big Momma told her all about the church. As Sassy learned the history, she felt really proud that her church was started by a Black man, Bishop Richard Allen, in 1794 in Philadelphia. Sassy found it amazing that more than 2.5 million members of her church live on five of the seven continents. She could go on vacation anywhere and find an AME church!

Sassy and Franklin participate in many of the church's youth activities, socializing with their friends and making new ones. Franklin met his friend Dontay at Vacation Bible School. Sassy's best friend in the whole wide world is Patrice, whom she calls Patty Cake. Patty Cake and Sassy met Rosa, their first Hispanic friend, at Vacation Bible School. They liked Rosa right off because she could speak two languages. By the end of Vacation Bible School, they were speaking Spanish, too.

Big Morning Star African Methodist Episcopal Church is very important to Sassy and her family—and that's a big family because it includes *all* their friends, too!

Chapter 1

My name is Mary Margaret Fanson. My grandmother, Big Momma, calls me "Sassy" because she says I'm "precocious." It's a new school year in this small tight-knit community. Franklin and his friends are middle-schoolers, and I am now in the fifth grade. After making it through the first semester, we are now in the middle of our winter break—also called Christmas Holiday in some schools. It does not matter what it is called; we just know we are out of school for at least two weeks.

The best part of Christmas is sharing it with the family and all our church friends. Patty Cake and I help bake cakes and cookies for the big Christmas meal, then spend hours at the mall shopping for just the right gifts. We still have more baking to do when we return. While we are inside with Big Momma, Franklin and his friends—Manuel, Dontay, and Gerald—help decorate the outside of the house. My friends and I have loads of fun during the two-week break from school.

Christmas comes and goes at the Fanson house. All the gifts are warmly received. The dinner prepared by my mother, Gloria Fanson, and Big Momma is, as usual, spectacular: roasted turkey, dressing or stuffing, baked ham, cranberry sauce, giblet gravy, sweet-potato casserole, green beans, corn on the cob, Watergate Salad, stuffed eggs, hot buttered Parker House rolls, and of course sweet tea. The meal is topped off with desserts of all kinds: German Chocolate cake, three-layer coconut cake, lemon-iced pound cake, different kinds of cookies, and the best homemade candies you would ever put in your mouth. Everyone eats their fill and takes some home. That is just how my family rolls with holiday dinner. We prepare enough food for an army, and it is enough to last for days.

With Christmas behind us, it is time to look forward to the new year.

Chapter 2

The first Sunday of the new year comes quickly to Big Morning Star African Methodist Episcopal Church. Like every Sunday, my family and I dress, eat breakfast, and off we go to the best church in the whole wide world. As soon as Franklin and I can, we meet up with our friends for church school. Franklin goes with his friends Manuel, Dontay, and Gerald to their class. Patty Cake, Rosa, and I go to our class.

We had learned so much church history last year that our teacher cannot think of any questions we cannot answer. Ms. Destiny, the YPD Director, calls us little history detectives . . . uncovering secrets and history and learning about our church. Big Momma just calls it, "being a good AME," knowing your heritage. I am so proud when she says that.

I am glad Big Momma had helped motivate and teach me and my school-friend Gerald all that history. Now I can really say with pride, "I Am AME!"

On the first Sunday, everyone remains in the sanctuary for Communion, which means no church school. We all hear an announcement about the upcoming meeting of the YPD, which is the Young People's Division in the AME Church. YPDers of all ages meet on the same Saturday the Women's Missionary Society (WMS) meets. We learn about the traditions of the AME Church—how to serve others and serve God. We learn the duties and responsibilities of the officers of an organization, like what the president and secretary are supposed to do. Then one day we will be prepared to serve in those positions. But right now, we just like attending and spending time with our friends. We have lots of fun, too. We play games, sing songs, and do arts and crafts.

Sister Willingham approaches the podium, walking firmly with the *clickity-clack* of her heals on the tile floor. She is one of the oldest members of the church. She knows everything about everything, and she does not mind correcting you about anything. Not only is she the coordinator for all Founder's Day events, but she is also the church secretary. She must have twenty bracelets on each wrist, 'cause they make the most annoying sound at the microphone. She adjusts them so they'll be quiet. Now, she coughs a loud, scraggly cough, then clears her throat, straightens her bifocals on her nose, shuffles the papers in front of her, and says authoritatively, "Young people! Young people! Your attention please! This announcement is for you. There will be a YPD Meeting this coming Saturday at 10:00 a.m. sharp." We all listen carefully. "All young people will be expected to attend." That being the final announcement. Sister Willingham collects all her papers, says, "Thank you," and turns to leave the podium.

Rosa and Patty Cake turn quickly to look at me, and we all show wide grins and clap silently.

"Yeah! We get to be together this coming Saturday at 10:00 a.m. sharp!"

Chapter 3

*F*riday night before our first YPD Meeting of the new year, I am in my room getting my clothes ready for Saturday. The YPD colors are green and white, so on a hanger and ready to wear when I get up is my green jumper and white long-sleeve turtleneck sweater to wear under it. I pack my church bag with pencils, markers, colored pencils, pens, and a notebook. *"I'm ready!"* I've already texted Rosa and Patty Cake to remind them to be on time. Patty Cake is always late if I don't remind her.

I step across the hallway into my brother's room and see him getting ready, too. He has laid out his blue jeans, a white shirt, and a green sweater vest to wear. Dontay and Manuel have FaceTimed him, and they are "pumped" to be spending Saturday together.

The Women's Missionary Society (WMS) meets at the same time, so we plan on going with Big Momma when she leaves for her meeting. Of course, Big Momma is ready. She has had her winter-white suit and her blue shoulder wrap ready since last Sunday.

Saturday morning, the house is full of motion. Everyone is up stirring about, getting dressed, and eating breakfast.

"Sassy," says Big Momma, "you and Franklin need to meet me at the truck at 9:30 sharp. I don't want to be late for my meeting, so be on time. You hear?"

"Yes, Big Momma, I know I'll be on time. I don't know about Franklin."

"Well, if he doesn't want to get left, he better be at that truck at 9:30," says Big Momma sternly. "Maybe you should remind him."

"Yes, ma'am, I will remind him," I promise, shaking my head as she hurries into her room to gather her things. I always have to remind my older brother about being on time. *Why is that? He's the oldest—he should be reminding me!* But never mind. I just want to make sure I am in the truck when Big Momma pulls off.

The drive to the church is only thirty minutes if we take the highway, and Big Momma insists on going the fastest route. She likes driving fast even though Daddy has warned her about going over the speed limit.

We arrive at Morning Star just in time. Franklin and I see Ms. Destiny LaShay Overton, the YPD Director. She says we can just call her Ms. Destiny. She's cool. She likes working with kids and we like her, too.

We run over to greet her. "Can we help you, Ms. Destiny?"

"Why of course. You kids are so sweet."

We grab bags and boxes from her car and help her get inside to the classroom.

"Just put everything on the table. We will be using some of those things for arts and crafts."

We all assemble in the Youth Center. The meeting is called to order by Ms. Destiny and turned over to the YPD Officers. The prayer is said, the scripture is read, and we sing a few songs. The roll is called, the agenda is approved, and the YPDers move on with the business meeting.

Ms. Destiny says, "Okay, YPDers, it is time to plan our events for the month of January and February. As you know, February is Black History Month. So, we really want to plan something special. Put your thinking caps on and let's come up with something really creative."

Franklin raises his hand. "Ms. Destiny, what about January? What are we doing to celebrate MLK Day—Dr. Martin Luther King, Jr. Day?"

"Franklin, I'm glad you asked. This year we're going to participate in the Martin Luther King Day Parade downtown."

Our eyes grow as big as saucers! Wow! What? Rosa, Patty Cake, and I look at each other and squeal silently to ourselves with joy!

"That's a great idea!" said Manuel. "We can decorate a truck with balloons and posters and have the name of our church on the side. We could either ride in the back or walk along with the truck."

"That sounds like a fabulous idea, Manuel," Ms. Destiny says.

"Then we're all going to the Annual MLK Breakfast at the event center downtown. The church is sponsoring us, so we all can go together. You'll have to dress up since this is a special occasion."

"Oh," Patty Cake says, "we won't mind dressing up for this event. We know we're supposed to represent our church well at special events."

"Can we wear our green and white?" asks Rosa.

"Rosa, I think that would be a great idea. Then everyone will know we're together and we're from Big Morning Star AME Church."

I say, "I've been wanting to go to that breakfast for a long time to see who's there and hear the speeches."

"Well, you'll get your chance this year," says Ms. Destiny. How many of you plan on going?"

Everyone's hands shoot up in the air. They were waving and shouting, "I'm going! I'm going!"

Ms. Destiny is excited to see that most all the kids are planning to attend. She knows for certain Mary Margaret and Franklin will be going, and they would encourage the others to attend. They are a tight group, so where one or two go, the others follow. I am just pleased that they always make good choices and lead in a positive way.

Ms. Destiny is writing names on her legal pad so she will have an accurate count.

"Okay. Let me make sure I have everyone." Ms. Destiny looks around as she calls each name from her pad. Each person says, "Yes."

When she calls Rosa's name, Rosa says, "Si!" Patty Cake and I giggle and follow Rosa's lead. When our names are called, we also say, "Si!" and high-five each other.

Ms. Destiny smiles a little, too, and finishes calling the names. "There. I have my count for the January breakfast. I will make sure there are enough seats available at the same table so we can sit together." She smiles at us again, clearly proud of our enthusiasm.

"So, those are the plans for January. Have you thought of anything for February?"

"Maybe we should go on a field trip to a museum or some special historical site," says Franklin.

"Or we could volunteer at a soup kitchen or deliver meals to people," offers Dontay.

Shelia suggests, "We could fix toiletry baskets for the homeless people in our community."

"Well, those are all good suggestions," agrees Ms. Destiny, "and yes we could choose one of the three to do—but I have another suggestion that would fit the occasion of Black History Month perfectly."

We know it will be something important. So, we get really quiet and lean in.

"What is it, Ms. Destiny? We want to know," says Franklin.

"You know, boys and girls, you don't always learn our history in school. The books that you have don't always discuss and tell our story the way we could tell it. So, we must research and find out the truth about our people and our heritage, sometimes on our own. Just like you had to study and learn the history of the AME Church, you have to learn the history of your people on your own. We have to be like super detectives, searching and uncovering hidden secrets of our ancestry. We have to search out the facts, just like this one detective that used to be on TV a long time ago would say, "Just the facts, ma'am." Ms. Destiny says impersonating Joe Friday from the old *Dragnet* TV show. The kids all laugh.

"Ms. Destiny, that's old-school—back in the day when all the shows were in black and white," says Gerald jokingly.

"Yes, Gerald. That was back in the day."

We all looked puzzled, confused. What? What is she thinking? Then, Franklin says, "So, Ms. Destiny, what do you want us to do?"

"I would like for you YPDers of Big Morning Star to research, write, and present the story of a historical African American or historical event affecting African Americans. You can choose who or what you'd like to research, but it has to be someone other than Martin Luther King, Rosa Parks, or Richard Allen. I want you to become "History Detectives!"

"History detectives?" Gerald says, confused. "What do you mean by that?"

"Well, I want you guys to research and find out information like a detective would. Look for the facts. Find the background story; uncover the secrets or little-known facts on the persons or events you choose."

"Oh. Okay! I get it! History detectives! We can do that!" Gerald says, feeling more confident about the assignment.

"No problem—that's easy," says Manuel, looking up from the notebook he was making notes in.

I announce, "I think I already know who I want to research."

"Me, too," chimes in Rosa.

Ms. Destiny smiles approvingly, "Oh, I'm so excited! I can't wait to see your work! Sunday, I will give you some guidelines to help you write your reports. You will have a month with a deadline of February 14th. Why do you think February 14th is the deadline?"

"Because that's Bishop Richard Allen's birthday, and he was the founder of our church—the AME Church," Sassy says proudly.

"Oh, Sassy. You remembered. Your grandmother will be so proud."

I just beam with pride. Big Momma *will* be proud of me.

Chapter 4

After leaving the meeting and picking up some pizzas for dinner, everyone goes to my house. Manuel, Dontay and Gerald arrive first. Rosa and Patty Cake arrive about ten minutes after them. Dontay, Manuel, and Gerald go to Franklin's room. Rosa and Patty Cake end up in my room.

Patty Cake and Rosa love my pink-and-yellow bedroom. The wallpaper is pink and yellow. The bedspread and fluffy pillows are pink and yellow to match the fuzzy throw rugs on each side of my bed. Most of our time is usually spent sitting in the window seat, relaxing among the overly stuffed pillows and cushy, stuffed plush toys.

We all want to begin thinking about who or what we are going to research for the reports. Rosa and Patty Cake are definitely going to choose a woman. Would it be a sports personality like Simone Biles, the Olympic gymnast, or Serena Williams the "GOAT"—greatest of all-time tennis player? Would it be a political figure like Michelle Obama or Representative Val Demings of Florida. I have seen Representative Demings on TV. I found out she is AME. She goes to the top of our short list. Or would it be Vice President Kamala Harris? Each of us has to choose someone, so we decide to be fair and draw. Patty Cake writes the names on slips of yellow paper and puts them in my hat. They each take turns drawing a name from the hat. Patty Cake pulls Michelle Obama's name. Vice President Kamala Harris is drawn by Rosa.

It is my turn to draw, but I'm thinking about something else. We are supposed to be detectives, so I decide to choose a topic I've wondered about but don't really know the answer. Did Bishop Richard Allen have any children? What happened to them? I share my idea.

"Wow," says Patty Cake. "I like that."

"What?" Rosa asks. "He never had children?

"Well, surely he had *some* kind of family, so that's what I intend to find out."

Patty Cake and Rosa are excited, chattering about their presentations, so I slip over to my brother's room to see if they have started deciding who to present.

I stand in the doorway of Franklin's "blue room." Dontay calls it the blue room because it is painted blue. They especially like all the model airplanes hanging from the ceiling. Franklin sits on his bed, while Dontay sits across from him at the desk. Gerald and Manuel had taken seats in the bean bag chairs on the floor. They are talking loudly, totally ignoring me.

"What about that guy in the movie we saw about the *Emanuel 9*?" Franklin says. "You remember? He was a slave that started the Emanuel AME Church in Charleston."

"Oh yeah, I remember the movie. His name was something like a foreign country—like Sweden or something," Franklin says, looking puzzled.

"You mean Denmark." Gerald shakes his head and rolls his eyes.

"Yeah, that's it—Denmark Vesey," Manuel says. "He would be a good person to research."

"And then there's one more—" adds Dontay. "Senator John Lewis from Georgia. You know he just died. He was *really* important. There would be lots of information on him."

"I remember his funeral," Gerald says, throwing his hands up in an exaggerated gesture. "It lasted about two or three weeks."

"It just seemed like it did," Franklin says, rolling his eyes in exasperation with his friends. "Hey, I saw Representative Val Demings on TV talking about being a proud AME. Maybe I could learn more about her."

"But she's a woman," Gerald says.

"I can think of lots of women who were just as important to our history as the men."

"Well, sure. Yeah," Gerald says.

Manuel adds, "I think it would be cool to learn about Representative Demings."

"Well, we have to decide who's going to do whom," Franklin says. "Do we need to draw straws or pull names out of a hat?"

"Naw, man—we'll just use the first letter of our names," Manuel offers. "So, that means Dontay goes first, then Franklin, Gerald, and then I'll be last."

"Hope you don't mind being last, man," says Franklin.

"That's okay with me." Manuel is writing names on pieces of paper. "That will work."

In the end, Dontay chooses Denmark Vesey; Gerald chooses John Lewis; Manuel picks Barack Obama, the former president; and Franklin draws... Representative Demings!

"Now that we know who we're going to research," Franklin says, "we have to make sure we get everything done by the deadline."

The other two spoke up. "That's right. We can do it."

"When did Ms. Destiny say she would give us the guidelines?" Dontay asks.

"Don't you remember?" I tease.

Ignoring her, Manuel explains, "She said she would give them to us on Sunday—tomorrow, man. What were you doing when she was talking?"

Franklin adds, "He was probably looking at Stacey and hoping she would look his way."

"Aw, come on, guys. I was listening, I just didn't remember. And besides, Stacey did look at me. She even winked and smiled." Dontay put his finger to his chin and tilted his head, then smiled. "How ya like me now, boys! Y'all just mad. Don't hate the playah; hate the game!"

All four of them just fall to the floor, laughing, teasing, and lightly hitting one another.

I just make a rude noise and tell them, "You boys won't impress anybody unless you get to work."

Chapter 5

$\mathcal{F}$ ebruary 14th, the deadline for the Black History Month research reports, is six weeks away—plenty of time to do a simple research paper. We are prepared to start the work according to Ms. Destiny's full page of guidelines:

> The paper has to be at least two doubled-spaced pages using nothing larger than 12-point font. You must provide a picture of your subject to go along with the report. You also have to prepare a five-slide PowerPoint presentation for the February YPD meeting.

That is asking a lot, and we are not even getting a grade for this. This is for church, not school. But as Ms. Destiny explains, this is one of those lessons that will last longer and be more meaningful than a grade. We just hope she is right because we also still have our homework assignments to do.

Another guideline Ms. Destiny shares with us is that we are not competing against one another for a prize or award. "Not everything is for a prize," she says "Some things are done to increase your knowledge, and those opportunities are priceless."

Rosa, Patty Cake, and I text and Zoom during the week on our progress, then get together on the weekend to talk about our research. The boys do the same. Everyone is working hard because we want our reports to be the best. We do not want to disappoint Ms. Destiny.

My friends and I had learned how to write a research paper in school. So, we take those same skills and apply them to this project. First, we start working on our outlines. After that, we start gathering our resources, taking notes, and putting things in order. We have to finish the paper before starting on the PowerPoint presentation; that would be the easy part. We had done those in school, too.

I talk with Big Momma about my choice to research.

Big Momma asks, "Well, baby, how are you going to find the information for your paper?"

"Oh that's easy, Big Momma. Everyone can use the internet to find most everything about a famous person, or a place or a subject."

"That's just so convenient. You can do most, if not all your research at home on your laptop. When I was in school, I had to go back and forth to the library and sit and write notes for hours because you could not take the reference books out. Things have certainly changed for the better. Y'all should be the smartest kids on the block. You have everything at your fingertips. All you have to do is ask Google or Alexa or that other girl—what's her name?"

"You mean Siri." I giggle at Big Momma.

"Yeah, Siri," Big Momma says laughingly. "They know everything. Those girls are almost like Sister Willingham. They know everything about everything."

"Oh, Big Momma, you're so funny. I guess you are right. We are lucky."

"Yes, baby," says Big Momma confidently. "Well, just make sure you take advantage of all those opportunities to learn. Not every kid is as blessed as you, Franklin, and your friends."

"Yes, Big Momma, we know."

Chapter 6

It has been a rough week. Every teacher gave assignments for homework. That's okay. I don't mind. I love homework. Reading, history, science, and language are my favorite subjects. I can complete those assignments with my eyes closed. Math is a different ballgame. I really have to study my math skills. When I need help, I don't mind asking my mother. She's a wiz at math. She knows just how to explain the problems so I can understand how to solve them.

Once I finish my homework, I can spend time on the YPD report. Patty Cake, Rosa, and I discuss our projects during lunch and plan to get together on the weekends. We agree to meet at my house on Saturday at 1:00 pm. By then, all the chores will be done, and I will have time to spend with my friends.

I usually sleep late on Saturday mornings, but this Saturday I get up early, fix my breakfast, start my chores, and finish by noon. I have just enough time to do a little work on my report before the girls arrive.

Franklin decides to sleep in, even though his friends are coming over. He has to hurry through his chores, and by the time he finishes, the boys are at the front door.

Patty Cake and Rosa go straight to my room. The boys stay downstairs with Franklin. Everyone has their laptops so we can all work separately on our reports.

Rosa starts sharing all the information she found on Vice President Kamala Harris. She says she found her to be quite interesting. I share that Bishop Richard Allen had a son named Peter who played the fife, but I'm still piecing together his story. We wait for Patty Cake to share her report, but she sits quietly on the pink and white area rug near my bed.

I prompt her. "Okay, Patty Cake, your turn. Tell us what ya got!"

She timidly smiles. "You guys are way ahead of me. I had so much homework to finish, I didn't have time to do anything on my report this week. You know how I am. I kinda get distracted. There was a program on TV I wanted to see. So, I watched that and then something else came up, and by Friday I had not done anything."

"How are you going to catch up by the 14th, Patty?"

"I don't know. I'm going to keep working on it. I know I can finish if I have just a little help. I just don't know where to start."

Rosa begins putting her things in her book-bag. "I have a lot of my research done. I can help you Patty Cake."

"Me, too," I add. "I think I'm on schedule, so I can help, too. What do you need us to do, Patty

Girl? We can help you get started, but we can't do all the work." I'm trying to be firm, patting Patty Cake on her shoulder. I move my stuff out of the way.

"Oh yes, I know that," Patty Cake assures us. "I would not want you to do everything for me. I just need a starting point."

"Right. So, let's get started. First you need to find some information on Mrs. Obama. We have magazines and books downstairs in the family room. We can find some interesting things to write about her. I'll get the books. Rosa, you help Patty Cake find pictures of Mrs. Obama online."

"Sure thing. We can do that, Sassy," says Rosa.

Patty Cake and Rosa move from the floor to the window seat. They open their laptops and log in. Rosa sits right beside her and tells her how to find the best images step by step.

When I come back, Patty Cake is shouting, "Yeah! That one! I like that one! She looks real pretty in that dress! Let's save that one!"

Rosa agrees. "I like that one, too! Do you know how to save the picture?"

"Si!" Patty Cake answers, nodding.

Rosa looks at Patty Cake and both girls fall over laughing.

"Girl, you are so funny," Rosa says, still giggling.

Patty Cake saves several pictures of Mrs. Obama for her report and starts looking through the material I brought upstairs.

"Now we're making progress!" I announce, trying to be encouraging. "I'll bet the boys haven't even managed to get started."

Chapter 7

*T*urns out the boys are working just as hard on their reports. I wander over and find Dontay, Manuel, Gerald, and Franklin with their laptops, note cards, and resources spread on the floor in front of them.

"Sassy, what do you want?" Franklin sounds like an annoyed big brother.

"Nothing. I just wanted to see how you fellows were coming along on your reports." I can't see what's on their screens.

Gerald closes his laptop quickly, blocking the screen. "We're doing just fine."

Franklin wants to maintain his privacy, too. "Just remember, Sassy, this is not a competition. So go away. I think I hear your girlfriends calling you."

I head back toward my room, but pause outside the door and keep listening.

"How you coming, Tay?" asks Franklin. "Tay" is what Franklin has been calling Dontay since they became friends. This happened after the incident at Vacation Bible School. Franklin made a special effort to become a better friend to Dontay after having bullied him last summer. Dontay appreciates the acceptance and treats the nickname as a show of friendship.

"I'm doing just fine, man," says Dontay. "I have my pictures and I'm starting on my report. I'm using all the notes from my note cards to write it. I just have to put them in order. What about you, Frank? Do you have your pictures?"

"Yeah, dude. Val Demings has lots of pictures, especially since she started running for office."

"That's like President Obama," Manuel says. "There are loads of pictures of him on the internet. The hard part is choosing just a few for my report."

Gerald announces, "I found plenty of pictures of John Lewis, too. I just chose three of him, one during the Selma to Montgomery March when he was young, one when he was first elected to public office, and one taken of him at the Black Lives Matter March before he passed."

"There were not a lot of pictures of Denmark Vesey," Dontay says. "The one I did find will be the one I use."

I slip back into my room but don't even get to sit down before we all hear Big Momma from the bottom of the stairs. "Anybody up there want some pizza?!"

Everybody stops and shouts, "I Do!"

Chapter 8

I always like to find time after school or on the weekend to spend with Big Momma. It's Saturday and Patty Cake is due to come over for help with her project. We learned in YPD meetings that it is our job as Christians to help one another. I certainly don't mind helping my best friend in the whole wide world.

This afternoon Big Momma and I sit in the sunroom waiting for Patty Cake. It's too cold now to sit outside like we did during the summer. So now we sit in the cozy sunroom right off the kitchen. A fire is roaring in the fireplace for this cold winter day. An overstuffed sofa and two chairs sit near the fire. Nice, thick, fluffy blankets are on each chair in case anyone needs one. Big Momma and I are waiting for Patty Cake to arrive as we sit at a game-and-puzzle table in the corner.

Big Momma says, "Sassy, how do you feel about helping Patrice with her project?"

"I would really feel bad if she did not finish on time when I could have helped her."

"Sassy, that is very admirable of you."

"Admirable is a good thing, right?"

"Oh yes, dawling. Admirable means something is to be admired or looked at as good."

"Okay, I think I got it: it's admirable to help someone."

"Oh, yes, baby dear. She will never forget you for that."

"I just think it's the right thing to do, Big Momma."

The doorbell rings, so Big Momma answers the door. "Hello, Patrice! Come on in. Sassy has been waiting for you."

"Thank you, Mother Fanson. It's good to see you." Patty Cake and Big Momma walk down the hallway to the sunroom. Patty Cake lays her coat and hat across the arm of the overstuffed sofa. She drops her book sack on the floor by the table. "Hey, Sass. Thank you for helping me out."

As Big Momma leaves the room, she asks, "Patrice, would you like some lemonade and teacakes?"

"Oh, no thank you. My momma says I can't have any tea or sodas because caffeine makes me hyper."

I roll my eyes and slap my forehead. "Teacakes are cookies, silly. They don't have tea in them. They are called teacakes because a long time ago ladies would eat them with their evening tea. Big Momma says it's an old-fashioned recipe. They're just sugar cookies. So, let's try this again. Would you like a sugar cookie and some lemonade?"

"Yes, please. I would love some lemonade with my teacakes," Patty Cake says with a flair of sophistication in her voice, her pinky finger extended, pretending to hold a cup of tea.

Both Patty Cake and I giggle and hug each other.

Big Momma disappears for a minute and returns with a tray holding two glasses of lemonade, napkins, and a small plate with six, round, lightly browned teacakes all neatly arranged. I take two cookies from the plate and so does Patty Cake. We each take a bite.

"Oh, man these are so delicious," exclaims Patty Cake. "And I don't taste any tea!"

I just grin and shake my head. "Patty-girl, you are so crazy."

Big Momma sits with us a while as we eat our teacakes and drink our lemonade. She starts telling us a story: "You know, Sassy, this reminds me of back in the day. When there was a need for the church to raise money, we would hold what were called High Teas or socials, like small parties. The ladies of the church, like the Women's Missionary Society or the Stewardess Board, would organize a high tea. It was usually held on a Sunday afternoon. All the ladies in the group would dress in their best Sunday dresses, their big "church lady" hats, and white gloves. Everyone would bring their best dish to the tea. Some ladies would make little sandwiches, like pimento cheese or cucumber. They would cut them into little triangles or circles. Mother Gardner was known throughout the community for her fancy cheese straws."

"Cheese Straws!" Patty Cake is fascinated. "What are cheese straws?"

"Cheese straws are like a baked, long, crinkly shaped cookie. They were so cheesy, crispy, and delicious. I'll have to make you some the next time you come over."

"They sound delicious. I love cheese. They don't have caffeine in them, do they?"

"No-o-o-o, Patrice!"

"And of course, there were teacakes and tea. The food was displayed on tables with white Battenburg Lace table clothes and silver candelabras. Everything back then was served on crystal or glass plates. No one would have thought of serving the delicious foods on plastic plates or in plastic cups. If you dared bring something in a plastic bowl or thought about serving food on a plastic plate, honey, you would've been talked about like a backslider with holes in your stockings!" Big Momma shakes her head and wags her pointer finger.

Patty Cake and I laugh until tears fill our eyes!

"This was a high-class event attended by the ladies and young girls of the church. The mistress of ceremonies would have arranged the entertainment for the high tea. Someone would read a poem. One of the young girls would do a special recitation. Mrs. Blackwell's daughter would always have to play a piece on the piano—" Big Momma leans closer and whispers as if someone might hear, "—even though she was not very good. We always clapped and encouraged her anyway."

"What did she play?" I ask.

"Oh, child that was so long ago; I don't hardly remember. I just know she missed a couple of notes here and there, but no one ever made fun of her. We just clapped and told her what a fine job she had done. And you know what, she is playing piano now for some big orchestra in New York City!"

Patty Cake and I look at each other and together say, "New—York—City!"

"So, all that practice really paid off. She really made her momma proud." Big Momma looks into the distance as if envisioning it all over again.

"Who knows?" Patty Cake adds, "She might be on *America's Got Talent* one of these days."

"Well, she just very well might be, Patrice. She's just that good now. And you know, I bet she would win." Big Momma winks and smiles. "Okay, girls, y'all better get to work. It will be dark soon." Big Momma leaves us to our work.

"I like hearing about things that happened long ago," Patty Cake says. "Your Big Momma knows a lot. And she can cook! Those teacakes were bomb-diggity! I could eat four or five more. Invite me over again—especially when she bakes those cheese straw thingies."

"Big Momma always bakes more than enough, so I'll fix you a to-go bag. And when she makes a big batch of cheese straws, you'll be the first one I call."

"You're the best friend in the whole-wide world, Sass." Patty Cake grabs me and squeezes tightly.

"Okay! Okay! I love you, too. Now let's get busy!"

Chapter 9

*W*inters in my city can be harsh. It is January with the expected bad weather: freezing rain, sleet, ice, and snow to the point of shutting down schools, businesses, and even church. We have four more weeks before the YPD reports are due, so we have to put on the speed. We still have to type the written report and create a five-slide Power Point. Ms. Destiny checks with each of us after church service to see how we are coming along. She is pleased to know that each of us— even Patty Cake—is on schedule to finish by February 14th.

The Martin Luther King, Jr., Day Holiday is this Monday. The YPD is preparing for the parade on Saturday. One of the men of the church, Brother Fletcher, was kind enough to allow us the use of his shiny new Ford F-150 pickup truck. We decorate it with paper flowers and garland. The sign on each side of the truck reads, *Young People's Division, Big Morning Star AME Church.*

We stand back and marvel at how beautiful the truck looks.

Franklin is the first to speak. "Man, that truck looks outstanding!"

"I second that motion!" shouts Dontay.

"If there was a contest for best-decorated truck in the parade, I know we would win," says Gerald.

"Well, there's not...a contest," says Patty Cake. "We did our best to show respect for Dr. King and pride in our church."

"I know that Patty Cake," Gerald says, trying to justify his statement. "I was just saying *if* there were a contest."

"Well said, Patrice. You're exactly right," says Ms. Destiny. "This looks perfect! I'm so proud of you." Everyone smiles and high-fives each other. "Okay, kids. Brother Fletcher is going to meet us downtown at Parking Lot K at 11:00 a.m. So go get dressed, and we'll all meet up there. Anyone need a ride?"

"No, ma'am. Our parents will get us there," says Manuel, running to catch up with the others.

Everyone arrives on time, dressed in their green-and-white attire. It is cold, so we are bundled up with scarves, hats, and gloves. Brother

Fletcher is waiting with the decorated truck. Rosa, Patty Cake, and I fuss with the flowers and the garland on the truck. We want to make sure everything stays in place. The guys help us girls into the back of the truck. Brother Fletcher had provided warm blankets in the bed to keep us warm while we ride in the parade. Ms. Destiny rides in the cab with Brother Fletcher.

The parade starts right at 11:00 a.m. Big Morning Star AME YPDers are about the fifth attraction in the parade. In front of us is the university band everybody is waiting to see. The band really gets the crowd stirred up and on their feet. When Big Morning Star passes through, people are still standing and clapping. We YPDers take it all in. It seems like the people are clapping for us, so we wave and smile even more.

By the time we return to the starting point, our hands and arms are tired from waving and our faces hurt from smiling so much. We get off the truck and begin taking the flowers, signs, and garland off Brother Fletcher's truck.

We thank him for allowing us to use his truck and make sure we leave it in good shape. He is happy that he could be a part of the parade and says he will be available next year if the YPDers want to be in the parade again. We are overjoyed.

Ms. Destiny has one announcement before everyone is dismissed to find our parents and go home. She says, "Was that not fun?"

We all say, "Yeah! That was lots of fun. Can we do it again next year?"

"We'll see. But for now, we have to think about Monday morning and the Martin Luther King, Jr., Breakfast. We'll need to meet at the center at 7:30 a.m. since it begins promptly at 8:00 a.m. Remember to dress in your green and white. A table has been reserved for us, so you don't have to worry about a seat. Everyone clear on what to expect on Monday? Are there any questions?"

"Oh no, ma'am. We get it," says Franklin.

"Yes, ma'am. We'll be there," exclaims Dontay.

"You don't have to tell me twice," Gerald shouts, patting his stomach and smiling, "—

especially if food is involved."

We all high-five each other again, hug, and say our good-byes. It has been a great day. The YPD from Big Morning Star AME Church has participated in its first King Day Parade. We are so proud.

Chapter 10

We YPDers from Big Morning Star AME Church arrive promptly at 7:30 am on the morning of the MLK breakfast. Dressed in our green and white, we wait patiently for instructions from Ms. Destiny. As she leads the way to our designated table, we follow behind her like little ducklings.

Each table can seat eight people, so we all sit together. The tables are set for breakfast with black linen table clothes and crisp white linen napkins. The silverware, glasses, cups, and saucers are on the tables, too. The centerpieces for each table are lit candles inside a hurricane glass container with flowers decorating the base. The candle gives a warm glow to our faces. The voice of Dr. King giving his speeches is playing over the speakers in the banquet hall as the people arrive and find their seats.

Once they are seated, everybody has a chance to look at their printed programs. It is really slick and glossy with a picture of Dr. Martin Luther King, Jr., on the front. Inside it lists what to expect today.

Patty Cake is sitting between me and Rosa. "Hey, Sassy, I sent you what I've got so far in my report to see what you think of the pictures. I'm having trouble picking which ones go best."

"Great. I'll take a look soon as I get home."

Patty Cake looks pleased. She checks her program. "This is going to be just like church. Look, there's an opening song, the scripture, and a prayer. Then the speaker speaks."

I joke, "They better be glad Brother Bailey, the minister of music, is not leading the song. You know he'd get happy and have everybody in here shouting."

Rosa and Patty Cake put their hands over their mouths to hide their laughter. They have to pinch themselves to stop. Rosa is giggling so hard the creases in the corners of her eyes are wet. Patty Cake pretends to cough to get her laugh out. They try to bring themselves under control after Ms. Destiny gives them the side-eye, but every time they look at each other they giggle again.

Finally, Ms. Destiny says, "Okay, girls, go on and get your giggles out before the program starts."

And we do.

The YPDers had attended big dinners at the church, but this one is over the top! This is a banquet with meals that will be brought out by servers, but first we have to listen to all the greetings, introductions, and speeches.

We are especially delighted to be at the breakfast because one of Big Morning Star AME's young members, Nelson Akim Ojebway is going to give the Youth Challenge. This is a brief speech given by a young person, calling all the young people to action, to live up to MLK's call to make the world a better place.

Breakfast is served, and it is delicious. The menu includes eggs, bacon, sausage, ham, grits, biscuits, pastries, juice, water, and coffee. We eat just about everything on our plates. We use our best table manners when passing the food. Ms. Destiny doesn't have to remind any of us to say thank you. Ms. Destiny is proud of us, and we are proud of ourselves, too.

After Nelson is introduced and approaches the podium, we clap and stand up. We are proud that one of our friends is giving the youth challenge. He does not disappoint.

We can tell he practiced his speech. He speaks with excitement and conviction, all without looking at any notes. He stands flat-footed and speaks as if he is Martin Luther King himself. When he finishes, the whole room erupts in applause. Everyone is on their feet, clapping and even whistling and cheering. Nelson gives a fantastic speech. We YPDers are proud of our church member.

As the event is closing, we wait for everyone to finish congratulating Nelson before we rush to hug him. He even poses for a picture with us. When the photographer says, "Smile!" we all give him our biggest and best.

Franklin shakes his hand. "Nelson, that was an awesome speech! You really did good, man!"

Nelson smiles broadly. "Thanks, guys! I was so nervous! My shirt is soaking wet from sweat. Did you really like what I said?"

"Nervous?" Ms. Destiny says. "We couldn't tell! Nelson, all that will soon pass. The more speeches you give, the more confident you will become. And who knows? Not only could you run for mayor, but you might also be the next governor!"

Gerald says, "Nelson, man, you really brought it! You really *should* think about running for mayor or something."

"Yeah," declared Dontay. "That would be great! Mayor—no, *Governor* Nelson Akim Ojebway! I like the sound of that!"

As we head out to the parking lot, Dontay adds, "Man, who knew Nelson could speak like that? He's always so shy and bashful."

Franklin says, "Yeah, he usually is, but he *brought it!* He was outstanding!"

Manuel teases him. "Franklin, you're going to have to find a new word besides outstanding. You're about to wear that one out."

"You might be right, Manuel, how bout *dope?*"

"Naw, man, that's not you. Stick with outstanding."

"Then outstanding it will be from this day until *eternity!*" Franklin runs through the parking lot and jumps into the air like a superhero. We laugh and run after him.

What a great time! The YPD from Big Morning Star AME Church has celebrated Dr. Martin Luther King, Jr., the whole weekend.

We will remember this weekend forever.

Chapter 11

The due date for the Black History reports is fast approaching. It is now three weeks before the big reveal, so my friends and I are working tirelessly to get everything accomplished. Every Sunday after church we gather in the fellowship hall to review notes and check in with each other. Franklin, Dontay, Manuel, and Gerald finished their reports and are now working on their Power Point slides. Rosa and I report that we are at the same place as the fellows. Patty Cake, however, is nowhere to be found, which is not like her. If Rosa and I are together, Patty Cake is right there with us.

Looking around the room, Gerald says, "Hey, Sass, where's your shadow, Patrice? I don't see her anywhere and that's not like her. She's usually stuck to you like ga-luue." He sticks his arm to his side mockingly.

"That's not true, Gerald, and you know it. But I do wonder where she is. She was in Children's Church this morning. She sat right beside me."

"See, what did I tell you?—stuck like glue."

"All right! All right! I hope she's okay. I think she might still be behind with her project and just doesn't want us to know."

Dontay says, "She knows she can ask us for help if she needs it."

Manuel agrees. "Yeah, Sass. You should call her when you get home and check on her. Let her know if she needs help, we'll jump right in and help her get'er done. We believe in *No friend left behind.*" He giggles and makes everyone else giggle, as well.

"Thanks, guys. I'll call her when I get home."

We say our good-byes and meet our parents to go home.

Chapter 12

Some Sundays Franklin and I ride with our parents to church, but this Sunday Franklin is going with our parents and I ride with Big Momma. I know it won't be long before we get home because Big Momma always takes the faster highway—and she *does* like to drive fast, even though Dad warns her about speeding. I'm glad this time because I am eager to get home and call Patty Cake.

Big Momma notices I'm being mighty quiet on the ride home. She looks my way several times, but I'm just gazing out the side window. "Sassy, baby, is everything all right?"

"Yes, ma'am. I'm just worried about Patty Cake. Gerald calls her my shadow. Well, my shadow was not there today, and I missed her. I hope nothing is wrong."

"Well, baby, I'm sure there's a simple explanation. Maybe her parents had to leave early, or she was helping Ms. Destiny in one of the classrooms. I'm sure she had a good reason. But there's only one way to find out..."

"Yes, ma'am. I plan on calling her as soon as I change my clothes. I have to find out what's going on."

I look out the side window of Big Momma's SUV again. I am worried and concerned. Big Momma pats my hand to reassure me that everything will be fine. I look lovingly at Big Momma and smile. If Big Momma says it will be fine...then fine it will be.

I need to get to the bottom of this mystery.

Chapter 13

"Hey, Patty Girl, where have you been? We waited in the fellowship hall for you. What's going on? Is anything wrong? Are you feeling okay?"

"Sass, to tell you the truth, I'm not feeling okay. I just could not meet you guys today. I was so embarrassed. I knew everyone would be talking about the reports and you—you just won't believe what has happened." Patty Cake's voice is breaking, and now she is starting to cry.

"Patty, what's wrong? Please don't cry. Tell me what's the matter. Maybe I can help. Please tell me." I wait patiently as Patty gathers her thoughts.

"Well, I was working on my report. I had my pictures and my written report all together on my laptop. I had even picked my five slides for the presentation and—and—just out of the blue, my laptop crashed! I lost everything! All my work! Gone!

I was so upset! My parents heard me screaming and crying, and they tried to calm me down, but I could not even sleep that night. It has been a terrible couple of days. And I just could not face you guys. So, I just went straight to the car." She is trying to cover her sniffles.

I can feel the sadness in my friend's voice. I have to do something to help her.

"Patty Girl, I am so sorry that happened. I know how hard you had been working on your report. I would have felt the same way had it been me."

"At this point, Sass, I'll just have to tell Ms. Destiny what happened and not give a report."

"No way, girlfriend! Nope! You can't throw in the towel! We still have time. We have at least a week and a half before the reports are due, but we need to get the others to pitch in and help, and I know they will." I'm thinking as I talk.

"Sass, do you think they would?" Patty Cake says with a little more confidence in her voice.

"I'm not ready to just quit. I want to finish my report like everyone else."

"Okay, here's what we'll do..." I say even as I'm still planning my strategy with Patty Cake.

Chapter 14

When we see Patty Cake the next day at school while gathering in the cafeteria for breakfast, everyone embraces her. Rosa, Gerald, Manuel, Franklin, Dontay and I sit at the table with her and try to reassure her that we are here to help.

Franklin speaks first. "Patrice, Sassy told us what happened. Don't be embarrassed. It could have happened to anyone. Heck, it could have happened to me. And I would have been just as messed up as you were."

"Yeah, Patrice," Gerald added. "I probably would have wanted to throw my laptop out the window if that had happened to me."

"Yeah, dude," Dontay joined in. "That was a real bummer." He sighed and looked around at the others for agreement.

"Okay," Manuel says. "So, Sassy told us the plan, and we're all in. You don't have to worry. We got you."

"Thanks, guys. You're going to make me cry. Thanks so much." Patty Cake hugs me and smiles at the others. "You guys are the best friends in the whole wide world!"

"Yeah, we know," Gerald says, folding his arms and posing like a rapper.

"Okay, enough already. Gerald, you are such a show-off," I say. "Okay, here's the plan. We'll meet at our house on Saturday morning and work all day if needed until we have Patty Cake's pictures and report in place. Deal?"

Everybody replies at once. "Deal!"

Chapter 15

At 10:00 am sharp everyone arrives at the Fanson house to work with Patty Cake on her report. Franklin and I have everything ready to welcome them. Everyone brings their laptops and settles in the sunroom where a warm cozy fire blazes in the fireplace.

Big Momma was expecting them, so she had been busy as well, preparing refreshments for the friends. On a large tray on a side table are freshly baked chocolate chip cookies and oatmeal cookies. When the time is right, she will offer them cups of hot chocolate.

I am sitting next to Patty Cake. Rosa is on my other side. As I open my laptop, Rosa says, "Sass, We should send our reports to each other so we have backups—just in case."

And just like lightning struck us, Patty Cake and I turn to each other and scream! "Aaaah!"

The boys and Rosa look shocked.

"What is the matter with y'all?" shouts Franklin. "What is it?"

Breathlessly, almost trembling, Sassy says, "Patty sent me the draft of her report! She doesn't have to start all over again!"

Patty Cake claps and jumps up and down, squealing with laughter. "I have the first version of my report! I know how to finish it again!" Patty Cake collapses in the middle of the floor, looking up at the ceiling and laughing. "My report is almost done!"

Rosa, Dontay, Manuel, Gerald, Franklin, and I all clasp hands and encircle Patty Cake. "We have the report! We have the report!" We *all* collapse into a pile on the floor. We are exhausted from our celebration.

Patty Cake says, "Now I know how Brother Bailey feels when the spirit hits him. This was an inspirational moment I'll always remember!"

We just laugh even harder.

Patty Cake is feeling great. She just needs to finish her slide presentation.

Big Momma comes in to see what the excitement is about. Even she has to cheer, hands raised high. "Praise God from whom all blessings flow!"

All the kids shout together, "Amen!"

Big Momma asks, "Okay, who wants hot chocolate?"

"I do! I do!" We all fall into the soft fluffiness of the overstuffed sofa and chairs.

Chapter 16

We are doing the final preparations for the presentations on February 14th, Bishop Richard Allen's birthday. Ms. Destiny had arranged a rehearsal for Wednesday night. She wants everyone to feel comfortable making their presentations and knowing exactly what to do.

When we arrive in the sanctuary on Wednesday night, the microphones have been set up and chairs put in place. Ms. Destiny has already given the media team a copy of everyone's PowerPoint presentation. Mr. Washington has loaded the slides into the projection program and is ready to follow along with the presenters.

We kids take our seats as Ms. Destiny steps to the podium. "Attention please, everyone. I'm going to go over the final instructions for Saturday's presentation. You have worked very hard on your reports, and I want everyone to be proud.

Just remember, you're not doing this for a grade, and this is not a competition. This is a learning experience. And I hope you learned more about your chosen personality than you knew before. Each of you will have ten minutes to present a summary of your report and your five slides. You will come to the podium as you're listed on the program. Brother Washington has a program, so he will know who's presenting. He'll project your slides when you give him a nod or say, 'First slide, please.' When your last slide has been shown, close with a brief statement or comment, say thank you, and take your seat. Any questions?"

"How long should our comments be, Ms. Destiny?" Dontay asks.

"Dontay, that's a great question. Comments or final statements should only be one or two sentences. Don't try to add to your report or tell everything you learned. Let your slides and your reports speak for you. Any more questions?"

Everybody replies in unison. "No ma'am."

"All right then, we're ready to begin our rehearsal. I'll come up first and greet everyone and give them some background information. I'll tell them that the purpose of the reports was for each participant to learn more about other historical African Americans besides Martin Luther

King and Rosa Parks. I'll let everyone know that each of you chose your own subject, did your own research, wrote your reports, and developed your own slide presentations. After I say all that, I'll turn the program over to Nelson Akim Ojebway. You all remember Nelson from the Martin Luther King Day Breakfast, right? Well, he's going to introduce you. Here is the order in which you will come to the podium and give your report:

"Manuel .... Former President Barak Obama

Gerald .... The Late Senator John Lewis

Patrice.................... Former First Lady Michelle Obama

Rosa....................... Vice- President Kamala Harris

Dontay .... Denmark Vesey

Franklin .... Representative Val Demings, and

Mary Margaret........ Peter Allen

"Everyone got it? Any questions?"

"Yes, ma'am. We have it."

While Ms. Destiny talks with Nelson, the others are talking quietly to each other.

"Man, I didn't know I was going to be first," says Manuel with some hesitation.

"Bro, you got this," Dontay reassures him. "You're setting the tone for the rest of us. This is your time to shine."

"Okay. Yeah man! I got this," Manuel says confidently. "This is just a rehearsal."

"Just do it!" Gerald says, leaning back in a gangster pose.

"Isn't that for sports?" I ask, giggling.

Franklin answers, slapping him on the back. "It can be for anything. Okay, Manuel you're up."

Ms. Destiny steps up to the podium first to do the introductions. She introduces Nelson Akim Ojebway, who then introduces Manuel.

One after the other, we all head to the podium, make our presentations, share our slides, thank the audience, and take our seats.

At the end of the rehearsal, Ms. Destiny gathers us around her for a group hug. "You guys make me so proud! You were excellent! I can't wait until Saturday!"

"Ms. Destiny," Patty Cake says, "did you really like our reports? What about the slides? Were they good?"

"Patrice, I could not have done any better myself! Everything was fantastic! And the slides were perfect."

Patty Cake looks at me with a smile as wide as the ocean. She just beams. All her hard work has paid off.

I hug her tightly and say, "I knew you could do it!"

The first rehearsal is done. Everyone starts gathering their things to go home. Now, time to prepare for Saturday morning, the YPD Meeting and the African American History Month Program.

Chapter 17

When I get home from Wednesday-night rehearsal, I find Big Momma sitting in the sunroom by the fireplace. I sit with her.

"Sassy, wouldn't it be nice to have a High Tea Party with all the fixings for the children after the African American History Program?" Big Momma must be remembering how fascinated Patty Cake and I had been as she told us about the church High Tea Parties the ladies used to hold back in the day. "That's part of our heritage as well, and I'm sure the children would enjoy some refreshments after the program. So, how shall I go about making this happen?"

Soon enough, Big Momma is on the phone with the members of the Women's Missionary Society planning an old-fashioned High Tea Party with all the fixings for Saturday. She calls Mrs. Gracey Perkins, the WMS president, to confirm the plans. She puts it on speaker so I can hear.

Sister Perkins is ecstatic! "Oh, yes, Mother Fanson! I miss those old days when we would gather and sing songs and share fellowship. I love the idea of sharing that part of our history with the young people. What can I bring?"

"Well, I just started planning and have not gotten to a menu yet. But I'll let you know."

"That sounds just fine! Fine indeed!" Sister Perkins says. "You can count on me!"

"She's right," Big Momma tells me. "I have to come up with a menu. That won't be hard. Let's see, we'll have small sandwiches—pimento cheese, cucumber and dill, and chicken salad—a cheese and cracker tray, stuffed eggs, grape-jelly meatballs, sausage balls, ham sliders, a fruit tray, vegetable tray, candied pecans, mixed nuts, pastel butter mints, petit fours, teacakes, and of course cheese straws. And to drink, hot tea, hot apple cider, and a fruit punch.

Big Momma gets busy making calls to her friends and members of the WMS. All of them agree to host a party for the YPD Members after the program on Saturday.

"Oh, yes, Mother Fanson," says Sister Brotherton cheerfully. "I will be glad to bring all the table coverings. I have the lace tablecloth and the real plates and cups. Sister Betty has the silver candelabra we used in years past. I know she'll be delighted to bring it. Oh, and don't forget to call Sister Malone; she still has those dainty little embroidered napkins we used. What a great idea. I'm so glad you thought of this. The kids will love it."

I can hear the smile on her face through the phone. Sister Brotherton is always so pleasant and so willing to do special activities for us kids.

Big Momma is finishing up her last call when the back door opens and Franklin enters the kitchen laughing and talking.

"What are you so fired-up about?" Big Momma asks.

"Ms. Destiny said we did an excellent job on our reports and presentations," he reports.

"That's right," I say, moving my bookbag to the chair by the table. "She said she was proud of us!"

"Yeah, Big Momma," Franklin continues, "we really did good—even Patty Cake. When it was her turn, she stepped right up to the podium, gave her report, and shared her five slides. She was so proud of herself, and we were happy for her."

"I'm glad you all were willing to help her with her report. Just think how that made her feel.

She will treasure the friendship she has with you forever." Big Momma gives me and Franklin an approving wink.

"What have you been doing, Big Momma," Franklin asks, "while we were at rehearsal?"

"Oh, you'll see on Saturday. It's a surprise!" Big Momma has a mischievous look on her face.

Franklin and I rub our hands together. "Oooooo! I can't wait!"

"Well, you'll have to. Now, go on up and get to bed. Tomorrow is another school day."

"Good night, Big Momma."

"Good night, babies. Big Momma loves you."

Chapter 18

Today is Saturday, February 14th, Valentines' Day, and Bishop Richard Allen's Birthday. Today is also the African American History Program at Big Morning Star African Methodist Episcopal Church. All the YPDers are present in their green and white. Ms. Destiny rounds up everyone for a last-minute pep talk. Rosa, Patty Cake, Franklin, Dontay, Gerald, Manuel, and I had arrived early. We greet the other kids as they arrive. The sanctuary is filling up fast. We did not realize so many people would come. We're getting a little nervous when we see the Pastor and First Lady arrive and take their seats. Things really heat up when the presiding elder and the bishop show up.

"Who invited them?" Gerald asks, speaking of the presiding elder and the bishop.

Franklin turns to Gerald and says, "They can come to any church they want to at any time.

They don't have to be invited. But I'm sure Ms. Destiny probably invited them."

Gerald boasts, "Well, kids, we better step up our game since we have celebrities in the audience."

"Manuel, now don't forget you're first," Dontay says. "You got this, man. You can do it."

"I got this. I can do it. I set the tone for the others," Manuel is saying under his breath. "I got this," he repeats as he fumbles with his presentation folder.

Everyone has taken their seats. Ms. Destiny welcomes everyone and gives them an introduction. She explains that we YPDers have been on a quest to uncover the history of other notable African Americans. We have become history detectives, searching out the facts.

When she finishes her introduction, Nelson Akim Ojebway approaches the podium to announce the order of the presenters. "Our first presenter is no stranger to any of us. Manuel will share what he learned as he explored the life and times of the 44th President of the United States, President Barack Obama. Manuel."

As Nelson takes his seat, Manuel comes to the microphone confidently and begins his presentation. "44th President Barack Obama was born in Hawaii—first slide, please."

A picture of President Obama in his official presidential portrait in dark suit with silver tie is shown, followed by a picture of him visiting the MLK Memorial, then a picture of him in the War Room during the assault in Iraq, then a picture of him dancing with First Lady Michelle Obama at the inaugural ball, then a picture of him with his daughters.

Manuel says, "This concludes my presentation. Thank you for your attention." All us YPDers clap enthusiastically for him, as does the audience.

Gerald approaches the podium with swagger. "The late senator John Lewis was always 'looking for good trouble,' and he found it. First slide please."

We see a young John Lewis marching on the Edmond Pettus Bridge in Selma, Alabama, then John Lewis standing with MLK during his "I have Dream Speech." The last slide shows John Lewis at the Black Lives Matter protest before he passed.

Gerald closes with, "I learned so much about this remarkable man. Thank you for your attention."

Patrice—Patty Cake—is next. Everyone is cheering her on, whispering, "You can do it!"

Patrice walks to the podium and begins sharing her report on former First Lady Michelle Obama. "First slide, please."

The first slide shows Mrs. Obama walking in the inaugural parade in her lime green coat dress. The second slide shows her playing with Bo and Sonny. The last picture is of her and the president dressed in formal attire for a special dinner.

Patrice takes one deep breath and says, "Mrs. Obama is a beautiful lady with class and style. Thank you for your attention." She walks quickly back to her seat and breathes a sigh of relief.

I grab her hand and squeeze it tightly and mouth the words, "You were so good."

Patty Cake just beams with pride.

Rosa is next with a report on Vice President Kamala Harris. "Kamala Harris is the first woman of color ever elected to the office of vice president. First slide, please."

Rosa talks through her five slides. At the end she says, "Vice President Kamala Harris has said that while she may have been the first, she will not be the last. Thank you for your attention."

Nelson Akim Ojebway announces Franklin Fanson as the next speaker.

My brother steps to the podium and begins his presentation on African Methodist Episcopal Church member and Representative Val Demings. "United States Representative Valdez—Val—Venita Demings represents the great state of Florida. Her district includes much of the area around Orlando and Disney World. Before she became a representative, she was chief of the Orlando Police Department—its first female chief. She is married to Mayor Jerry Demings. They have three sons. First slide please…"

Franklin introduces each of his slides of Congresswoman Demings, then finishes with, "And finally, Representative Demings is a proud member of St. Mark African Methodist Episcopal Church. Thank you."

He breathes a sigh of relief and quickly returns to his seat.

Dontay follows Franklin with his report on Denmark Vesey. "Denmark Vesey was one of several founders of what is now Mother Emanuel African Methodist Episcopal Church. He was a slave who bought his freedom with the winnings from a lottery, so in 1800, Denmark Vesey started the new century as a free man.[1] "First slide, please." Manuel showed a picture of Denmark Vesey. After showing all five slides. Manuel made a simple statement, thanked everyone, and returned to his seat.

I am the last presenter. I feel a little nervous, but I walk confidently to the podium. After arranging my presentation folder on the stand, I take a deep breath, clear my throat, and begin to speak. "As AMEs, we know a lot about Bishop Richard Allen, the founder of our denomination. As a matter of fact, today is his birthday. We know just a little more about his wife Sarah Allen, but we know very, very little about their children. Well, today, we're going to learn a lot about one of his children, as we uncover the secret life of *Peter* Allen.

"Peter Allen was born in Philadelphia, Pennsylvania, in 1805 to Bishop Richard Allen and Mrs. Sarah Bass Allen. In 1835 Peter Allen moved from Philadelphia, a city whose entire black population of approximately 15,000 was free, to Huntsville, Alabama, where only one percent of the state's black population enjoyed freedom. After arriving in Huntsville, he married an enslaved woman, Mary, who lived from 1807 to 1885.

"Beginning in late October 1835, appeals were published in several Alabama newspapers, including the *Huntsville Southern Advocate*, urging Alabamians to come to the aid of their 'brothers in Texas.' On the night of October 31, 1835, an organizational meeting was held in Huntsville, and a volunteer company was formed by Captain Peyton S. Wyatt. Although Peter was a free black who had only recently moved to the city, he was welcomed into the company as a flautist. The company departed Huntsville on Sunday, November 8, 1835."

Everybody is so quiet I have to look to make sure everybody is still here. They are focused on my every word. I have their full attention!

"Arriving in Texas in early December, Wyatt's company was put into service on December 25, 1835. On January 12, 1836, they were sent to Goliad, a fort in Texas. Allen's company participated in the Battle of Coleto Creek before they were forced to surrender on March 20, 1836. Peter Allen was imprisoned at Goliad, Texas.

"The night before the surrender, Captain Shackleford, commander of the Alabama Red Rovers, recalled that the musicians of the troop, which included Peter Allen, played the tune 'Home Sweet Home' on their flutes as tears rolled down many a manly cheek.

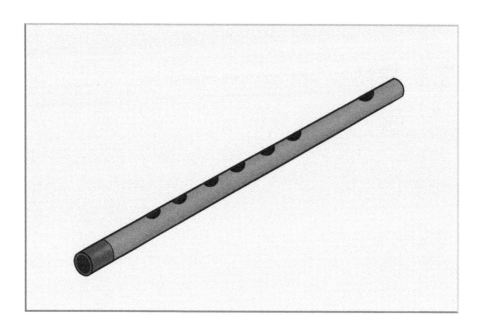

The next morning, Palm Sunday, March 27, 1836, the men were awakened at dawn by their Mexican guards. Santa Ana, the cruel Mexican president, came to Peter Allen just as the captured soldiers were about to be shot. He ordered Allen to play 'Home Sweet Home' on his fife so the soldiers could hear the beautiful music flowing in the air and die with deep regrets. 'Follow my orders, and I will spare your life, but the others will die.' After careful consideration of all he would be sacrificing, Peter Allen said, "No! I will not play. I will just die with the rest of the boys."

I hear quiet gasps and look up to see sad faces, a few with hands over their mouths. The words are hard for me to say: "Peter Allen, a hero we should all remember, died bravely that day along with his brothers."

I have to wipe a tear from my eye. Hankies and tissue are coming out of pockets and purses in the audience.

I take a breath and continue: "Peter's widow, Mary, eventually remarried a local man, Mr. John Cook, and lived the remainder of her life in Huntsville. After she died on June 23, 1885, her obituary recounted Peter's service in the Texas Revolution and his refusal to save his own life."

Everybody is still watching me. "That song has new meaning for me now, maybe for many of you, too. I'm sure Peter Allen was thinking of home, as were his brothers. Peter lived and died on his own terms, and that makes him a true hero.

"First slide, please." After sharing five slides representing the life of Peter Allen, I pause and say, "And finally, the secret life of Peter Allen, one of the children of our esteemed Bishop Richard Allen, has been revealed."

I collect my papers, close my folder, and thank everyone for their attention. I walk proudly back to my seat to enthusiastic applause, some rising to their feet, a few still wiping tears from their eyes. Others whistle and cheer like for a sporting event!

Franklin hurries over to embrace me, then waves at the audience to clap louder for an excellent presentation. Manuel, Dontay, and Gerald are jumping around, pumping their fists in the air, shouting, "Way to go, Sassy!" The girls are grinning, giving me thumbs-up!

Ms. Destiny heads to the podium and uses a tissue to wipe her eyes. "I knew this was going to be outstanding, but nothing like this magnitude. I don't know about you, but I'm just blown away with our young YPDers. Aren't they amazing?" The audience gives us all a standing ovation.

The Pastor comes forward to give his closing remarks and the benediction. He again asks the audience to applaud all of us YPDers.

After everyone settles down, the Pastor invites everyone to the fellowship hall for a special celebration for the YPDers hosted by the WMS. Friends and family are crowding around the stage to hug us and take our pictures.

"Come on you, guys!" I insist. "Let's hurry to the fellowship hall to see the surprise!" I lead the way.

"We're right behind you Sassy!" Patty Cake and Rosa say, almost out of breath.

The guys are coming, as well, and they're still bouncing from all the excitement.

"Wow, Sassy, you brought it!" Gerald says. "I had never heard of Peter Allen, but now I know. I don't know who I'd vote for mayor now, Nelson or *you!* You just gave him some stiff competition!"

"I'm not running for anything anytime soon. I'm just glad that it's over. I know how Nelson felt now."

We all get to the entrance of the fellowship hall at the same time. We stop short, and Patty Cake even bumps into me. We are all amazed at what we see!

"It's a High Tea Party!" Patty Cake and I squeal in unison.

"A what?" The fellows look at each other, puzzled.

"All I see is food. Tell me later what a High Tea is," says Gerald as he makes his way to the head of the line.

And a High Tea Party it is! Big Momma and the ladies of the Women's Missionary Society have all the fixings. The tables stretch the entire length of the huge fellowship hall. Each is dressed with real lace table clothes. The serving dishes are real glass or crystal, and the food is out of this world. Tiered plates and trays are stacked with small individual sandwiches. Trays are filled with petite fours, cheese straws and teacakes. Other dishes contain mints and nuts. Two huge crystal punch bowls sit at each end of the long tables. I have never seen so much food!

Rosa, Patty Cake, and I sit together with full plates.

Rosa asks, "What are these?" She holds up a small round cookie.

Patty Cake explains in her best British accent: "These, my dear, are teacakes. And don't worry, they're not made with tea, so you won't be hyper if you eat them."

Rosa and I glance at each other and laugh.

"Patty Cake, girl, you just kill me sometimes!" I say. "But I would not trade you for anything. You either, Rosa. You two are my best friends in the whole wide world!"

"Man," Dontay says, "these cheese straw thingies are the bomb! I could eat a plate full!"

We history detectives have achieved our goal: discovering the names and backgrounds of historical African Americans and uncovering the secret life of Peter Allen.

Big Momma and Ms. Destiny are off to the side smiling and talking. They both look my way, touch their hearts, and blow me a kiss. Tears are filling my eyes. I have never felt more proud, and I have never been prouder to say:

Sassy says here is where you can learn more!

Herb Frazier, Bernard Edward Powers, Jr., Majority Wentworth, *We Are Charleston, Tragedy and Triumph at Mother Emanuel* (W Publishing Group, 2016), 67-74.

Tyler, Mark Kelly. "Richard Allen's Son Found in Texas—How Could it Be?" markkellytyler. blogspot, (blog) December 2011: https://mark-kellytyler.blogspot.com/. If you do not see the article about Richard Allen's son, navigate through his posts to find December 2011.

Big Momma's High Tea Recipes

Forgotten Teacakes

Tip: Using a silicone pad or parchment paper will make baking cookies easy and clean up a breeze.

c.=cup   tps.=teaspoon

Dough

½ c. Butter Flavor Crisco	2 tps. baking powder
½ c. sugar	¼ tps. Baking soda
1 egg	¼ tps. Salt
1 tps. Vanilla	¼ c. buttermilk
2 c. all-purpose flour	¼ tps. Nutmeg

1. Heat oven to 375°F.
2. Combine Butter Flavor Crisco and sugar in in large bowl. Beat at medium speed of electric mixer until light and fluffy. Beat in egg and vanilla.
3. Combine flour, baking powder, baking soda and salt. Add alternately with buttermilk to creamed mixture at low speed. Mix well after each addition.
4. Roll dough to ½ inch thickness on lightly floured surface. Cut with round, floured cookie cutter. Place on baking sheet.
5. Bake at 375°F for 10-12 minutes.
6. Remove to cooling rack.
7. Serve warm or at room temperature.

Makes about 2 dozen teacakes.

The Black Family Reunion Cookbook. *Forgotten teacakes*. New York, New York. Simon & Schuster 1991. Pg. 190.

Cheese Straws

Tip: A cookie press with a cheese straw tip will be required.

Ingredients:

1-10oz. block of Cracker Barrel X-tra Sharp Cheese,
    Grated or a 10 oz. bag of grated X-tra sharp cheese

1 stick of butter (soften)

1 ½ c. plain, all-purpose flour

¼ c. corn starch

2 tps. baking powder

1 tps. salt

¼ tps. ground, red pepper

1. Mix all ingredients thoroughly by hand in a mixing bowl.
2. Place ½ of mixture inside cookie press with cheese straw tip attached.
3. Press long strips of cheese mixture onto cookie sheets.

4. Bake 350°F, 15 to 20 minutes.

Recipe may be mixed several times if a large amount of cheese straws is needed.

Yields: 2 ½ dozen of 8-inch-long cheese straws.

Big Momma's High Tea Recipes

About B. A. Johnson

Re tired educator B. A. Johnson is a lifetime member of St. John African Methodist Episcopal (AME) Church in Huntsville, Alabama. After 35 years spanning elementary classrooms to administration, she continues her passion in the church, working with the New Members Class for Youth, which requires her to adapt adult

materials for children. Recognizing the impor-
tance of young members understanding their
church history, she developed the characters
for the illustrated children's story *Sassy Discovers the AME Church* was born, which has grown
into a series with Sassy Uncovers Peter Allen's
Secret and she hopes more stories to come. Ms.
Johnson continues to hone her writing skills
as editor and contributor to the 27-year-old
St. John AMEN, a newsletter highlighting many
of the events, people, and activities of the local
church. Several of her articles have appeared in
The Christian Recorder, the official organ of the
AME Church since 1851. Find B. A. Johnson at
FreshInkGroup.com.

Fresh Ink Group

Independent Multi-media Publisher

Fresh Ink Group / Voice of Indie / GeezWriter / Push Pull Press

❧

Hardcovers
Softcovers
All Ebook Formats
Audiobooks
Podcasts
Worldwide Distribution

❧

Indie Author Services
Book Development, Editing, Proofing
Graphic/Cover Design
Video/Trailer Production
Website Creation
Social Media Marketing
Writing Contests
Writers' Blogs

❧

Authors
Editors
Artists
Experts
Professionals

❧

FreshInkGroup.com
info@FreshInkGroup.com
Twitter: @FreshInkGroup
Facebook.com/FreshInkGroup
LinkedIn: Fresh Ink Group

Young "Sassy" has always been proud to be AME, a member of her African Methodist Episcopal church, but why? Sassy enjoys learning during the Children's Church group, but that new boy knows more about AME than she does! With the help of her grandmother, "Big Momma," she discovers the real story behind the founding of AME. Along the way, she and her friends and her brother, Franklin, deal with bullying, kindness, death, grief, pride, forgiveness, and the very ideas of fairness and including others. They also confront the harsh reality of prejudice and hatred when a gunman attacks the Mother Emanuel Church in Charleston. In Sassy Discovers the AME Church, one little girl embraces the idea of belonging to something so important, and of proudly sharing her faith with everyone she loves.

Hardcover, Softcover, All Ebook Formats Worldwide!

by Helen Borel, PhD
A Place to Remember...

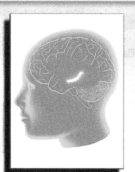

The Interactive
Brain Book:
Fun Learning for
Science Lovers

FreshInkGroup.com

Helen Borel, PhD
@BorelMedWriter

Lightning Source UK Ltd.
Milton Keynes UK
UKHW051540060123
414915UK00022B/71/J